# THE LIVES OF SAINTS

## LEIGH BARDUGO

ILLUSTRATED BY DANIEL J. ZOLLINGER

**[Imprint]**
MAKE YOUR MARK

A part of Macmillan Publishing Group, LLC
120 Broadway, New York, NY 10271

Library of Congress Cataloging-in-Publication Data is available.

ISBN 978-1-250-76520-8 (hardcover) — ISBN 978-1-250-80165-4 (special edition)

Our books may be purchased in bulk for promotional, educational, or business use.
Please contact your local bookseller or the Macmillan Corporate and Premium Sales Department
at (800) 221-7945 ext. 5442 or by email at MacmillanSpecialMarkets@macmillan.com.

Book design by Natalie C. Sousa
Illustrations by Daniel J. Zollinger
A special thanks to Fanni Demecs for her work on the cover.
Imprint logo designed by Amanda Spielman

First edition, 2020

1 3 5 7 9 10 8 6 4 2

fiercereads.com

As a wise woman once said,
"You know the problem with heroes and Saints?
They always end up dead."
In fact, we all end up dead.
But people who steal books
have a truly miserable afterlife.

**LEIGH BARDUGO** is a #1 *New York Times*–bestselling author of fantasy novels and the creator of the Grishaverse, which spans the Shadow and Bone Trilogy, the Six of Crows Duology, *The Language of Thorns*, and the King of Scars Duology. Her short stories can be found in multiple anthologies, including *Best American Science Fiction and Fantasy*. Her other works include *Wonder Woman: Warbringer* and *Ninth House*.
leighbardugo.com
grishaverse.com

**DANIEL J. ZOLLINGER** is an award-winning illustrator and painter. Born in Glens Falls, New York, and raised in Schenectady, he later earned his degree in art from the Art Institute of Pittsburgh. Dan cut his teeth as a Madison Avenue storyboard artist before transitioning to editorial illustration. His list of publications include the *New York Times*, the *Washington Post*, and *Esquire* magazine. He has had several one-man and group shows as a painter, and currently focuses on book illustration and painting. He resides in Holly Springs, North Carolina, with his lovely wife, Karen.

*To those who keep faith with stories*

# TABLE OF CONTENTS

# SANKTA
# MARGARETHA

As sometimes happens in Ketterdam, a demon took up residence in one of the canals, this time beneath a bridge in the Garden District. It was a hideous clawed thing with a scaly white hide and a long red tongue.

Each day children would pass over the bridge on their way to school and then back again on the way home, in two lines, side by side. They didn't know a demon had come to live in the city and so they would laugh and sing without worrying what attention they might attract.

One day, on their way to school, as the children stepped off the bridge and onto the cobblestones, they heard a voice whisper sweetly, "Jorgy, Jorgy, you'll be first."

Now, they did have a little boy named Jorgy among them, and he was teased mightily when they heard the voice singsonging, but no one thought too much about it. All day the voice whispered—following them through lessons and while they were at play: "Jorgy, Jorgy, you'll be first." But nothing happened, and so the children strolled home in their two orderly lines, hooting and giggling as they crossed the bridge.

When they reached the other side, Jorgy was nowhere to be found.

"But he was right here!" cried Maria, who had been beside poor Jorgy.

The children ran home and told their parents, but no one listened when they described the whispering voice. The families searched high and low, and took boats up and down the canal, but there was no sign of Jorgy. They were sure that some madman or criminal must be to blame and set guards all along the street.

The next day, as the children walked to school, Maria was afraid to cross the bridge. She heard a voice say, "Do not worry, I will hold your hand and no one will take you."

Maria thought it must be her friend Anna and so reached out to hold her hand. But when they arrived at the other side of the bridge, Maria found her hand empty and Anna was gone. The children wept and shouted for help, and their teachers and parents scoured all along the streets and waterways. Anna could not be found.

Again, the children told their parents of the whispering voice, but they were all too distraught to listen. Instead they doubled the number of guards.

The next day, the children walked quietly to school, huddling together as they neared the bridge. "Closer, closer," whispered the demon.

But in an apartment above a jeweler's shop, Margaretha was watching from her window. Her father sold all manner of beautiful things in the shop below, many of them Margaretha's designs. She had a gift for the finest details, and the stones she set were brighter and clearer than they had any right to be.

That morning as she worked in the square of sunlight by her window, she saw the demon leap up like a curl of smoke to seize little Maria. Margaretha shouted at the vile thing, and without thinking, she grabbed a sapphire in her hand and hurled it at the creature.

Light caught and hung on the jewel as it arced through the air, making it glitter like a falling star. The demon was transfixed. He tossed his prey aside and leapt into the canal after the beautiful jewel. Maria bounced along the cobblestones. She had a very sore bottom and a skinned knee, but she hurried on to school with the other students, safe and sound, and grateful she'd been spared.

Margaretha tried to tell her friends and neighbors about what she'd seen. They listened attentively, for Margaretha was a practical girl who had never been given to fancy. Yet no one quite believed her strange tale. They agreed she must have a fever and recommended she retire to bed.

Margaretha did go to her room and there she sat at her desk, vigilantly watching the bridge. The very next morning, when the demon tried to seize Maria again, Margaretha tossed a big emerald pendant into the canal. The demon threw Maria into a doorway and leapt into the water to retrieve the jewel.

Now, Margaretha knew this must not go on. One day she would be too slow and the demon would take another child, so she set her mind to the problem. She worked all night upon an extraordinary jewel, a diamond brooch so heavy she could barely lift it. As dawn broke, she used a pulley and a winch to raise the brooch off her desk and heft it out of her window, until it dangled above the canal, straining the rope that held it. In the shop below, her father's customers wondered at the noises coming through the ceiling, but with children disappearing right and left, there were other things to concern them.

This time, when the children approached the bridge, Margaretha was ready. As soon as the demon leapt up, she released the rope. The brooch plummeted into the canal with a tremendous splash. But even the quick glimpse the demon had of it was enough to drive him mad with need.

Down the demon went into the dark waters, all thoughts of children to devour abandoned, its claws reaching out for the diamond at the bottom of the canal. But the brooch was too heavy to lift. Anyone with sense would have left the jewel there, but demons have no sense, only appetite. It had seen the sparkle of the brooch as it fell and it knew this stone was more lovely and necessary than any it had seen before.

The demon died wrestling with the brooch, and its drowned corpse floated to the surface of the canal. The Merchant Council skinned its body and used its hide as an altar cloth at the Church of Barter.

It's said that many years later, when the great drought came and the canals ran dry, a stash of jewels was found at the bottom of the canal, including a brooch so heavy no one could lift it, and beneath that pile of gems, a heap of children's bones.

Every year, lanterns are lit along the canal and prayers are said to Margaretha, the patron saint of thieves and lost children.

# SANKTA
# ANASTASIA

Anastasia was a pious girl who lived in the village of Tsemna. Known as a great beauty, she had red hair bright as a field of new poppies and green eyes that shone like polished glass. This was what the villagers remarked upon when they saw her at market, whispering what a shame it was that Anastasia spent all her time lighting candles for her poor dead mother in the church and tending to her old father in their sad little house. A girl like that should be seen and celebrated, they said, and warned she would grow old before her time.

But the villagers lost their taste for gossip when Tsemna was struck down with the wasting plague. They hadn't the strength to go to market or even church any longer. They lay in their beds, gripped by fever. No food could tempt them, and even when they were force-fed, they withered and eventually died.

Anastasia did not sicken. Her father, afraid their neighbors would brand her a witch, kept his daughter in the house, hiding her plump limbs and rosy cheeks. But one morning her father would not rise from bed; he would eat neither meat nor bread nor any of the delicacies Anastasia prepared for him.

A voice spoke to her as she knelt by the bed, praying to the Saints for her father's life to be spared. When Anastasia rose, she knew what to do. She found her mother's sharpest knife, made a long, slender cut along her arm, and filled a dish with her blood. She lifted it to her father's lips and bid him drink.

"What is that delicious aroma?" her father cried. "It smells like partridge with crispy skin and wine warmed with spices."

He drank greedily of his daughter's blood, and soon his cheeks were flushed and the plague had gone from him. A servant had observed the whole endeavor, and word soon spread of the healing properties of Anastasia's blood.

The townspeople came to the house, then people from the neighboring towns. Anastasia's father begged her to see sense and bar the door, but she refused to turn anyone away. Her blood was drawn into little dishes—from her wrists, her arms, her ankles—and taken out to the people, who drank and were healed. When Anastasia learned that there were people too weak to come and beg for her blood, she asked to be placed in a cart, and she was taken into the countryside, from village to village, to farmsteads and cities. She grew weaker and weaker until finally, in Arkesk, the last drops of her blood leaked from her body into a waiting cup and her body became a husk that blew away on the wind.

Sankta Anastasia is known as the patron saint of the sick and is celebrated every year with tiny dishes of red wine.

# SANKT KHO AND SANKTA NEYAR

Long ago, before the reign of the Taban queens, Shu Han was ruled by a cruel and incompetent king. His many wars had left the ranks of his troops depleted and his country vulnerable; the draft had been exhausted and there were no more soldiers to fill the army's ranks. The king gathered his advisers, but all they could do was prepare for the enemy to descend.

A clockmaker named Kho lived in the shadow of the palace and he vowed to use every ounce of his skill to help protect the kingdom. He worked through the night, binding bone to metal, stringing sinew over cogs. In the morning, arrayed in neat lines, their boots and buttons shining, a battalion of clockwork soldiers stood at attention. When the enemy began their assault on the capital, the clockwork battalion marched into the fray. These soldiers never tired. They never grew hungry. No wound could break their stride. They fought on and on until the last of the enemy soldiers were dead.

But the king did not let them stop. He sent the battalion to claim territory to which he had no right, and if the people there protested, he ordered his clockwork soldiers to silence resistance to his rule. On the battalion marched, slaying all who dared offer challenge, laying waste to cities at the king's command. They marched until their clothes frayed and their boots wore away to nothing, yet still they did not stop.

At last, even the king grew tired of conquest and ordered the clockwork troops to halt. They did not. Maybe the clockmaker had not crafted them ears fine enough to hear the king's orders. Maybe the soldiers simply didn't care. Maybe their cogs turned more smoothly with blood to moisten their teeth. Or maybe, they could not stop. They had been made for destruction and had no choice but to see it done.

High on a hill, a nobleman's daughter watched the battalion approach her city, and like Kho, Neyar vowed to use every bit of her skill to protect her people. She went to the family forge, and there she fashioned a blade so sharp it could cut shadow and so strong it laughed at steel. Neyar whispered prayers over the metal and walked the long road down to the city walls. There she met the clockwork battalion. For three days and three nights, Neyar fought the unstoppable soldiers, her blade flashing so brightly the people watching swore she had lightning in her hands.

At last, the final soldier fell in a heap of blood and broken clockwork, and Neyar laid down her weapon. Then she demanded that their irresponsible king lay down his crown. A coward to the last and without soldiers to defend him, the king fled the country, and Shu Han has been ruled by queens ever since. The sword was dubbed *Neshyenyer*, Relentless, and can still be found in the palace of Ahmrat Jen. Its blade has never rusted.

Sankt Kho is known as the patron saint of good intentions and Sankta Neyar as the patron saint of blacksmiths.

# SANKT JURIS
# OF THE SWORD

In one of Ravka's many wars, a general marched his army into enemy territory, sure of a swift victory. But the weather had other ideas. The wind shredded through his soldiers' thin coats with cold claws. The snow crept through the leather of their boots, and their supplies dwindled. The enemy didn't bother with battles, but hid amid the rocks and trees, picked off the general's men in bursts of gunfire, and waited for winter to have its way.

Soon the army was less a body of men than a loose-limbed skeleton, staggering from dawn to dusk. The general abandoned his pride and called for a retreat. But by then, the final mountain pass that would lead them home was blocked with snow. The soldiers made camp as best they could. Night closed around them like a fist, and their fires sputtered as if struggling to draw breath.

The general railed against his luck. If only the winter had not come so soon. If only the enemy had not been ready. If only the pass had not been blocked. He cursed fate and told his men that if they died this night, taken by the cold, it would be because they had been abandoned by cruel and merciless Saints.

"Where is Sankta Yeryin to feed us? Where is Sankt Nikolai to guide us home? They're safe and warm some-where, laughing at their wayward children."

Some of the men agreed. They sneered at the Saints' names and spat into the snow. But in one tent, six soldiers gathered. They bent their heads and prayed to the Saint who they believed had kept them alive thus far: Sankt Juris, patron saint of the battle weary, the warrior who had bested a dragon through cunning and strength, who knew the suffering of long nights in siege, and who might hear the pleas of common soldiers.

Shivering in their frayed blankets, the six soldiers heard a distant flapping of wings and felt the earth rumble gently beneath them. Then, up through the ground, they felt a warm gust, an exhalation of heat, as if the mountain were no longer rock and snow but a living beast, a dragon with breath of fire. They fell into a deep slumber, their battered bodies warm for the first time in months.

When they woke, they found the general and the other men had frozen to death in the night. The snow had melted away from the mountain pass, and flowering amaranth lined the path, its long leaves like tongues of red flame, guiding the faithful soldiers home.

Every year on his Saint's day, the people honor Juris by placing bunches of red amaranth over their doorways and welcoming soldiers and veterans into their houses.

# SANKTA VASILKA

asilka was a gifted weaver who lived in a high tower at the top of a winding stair. The chamber where she worked her loom was surrounded by windows that filled the room with brilliant sunlight at every hour of the day. There, she wove cloth weightless as smoke in patterns of infinite complexity. Any thread she touched seemed to brighten in her fingertips.

A man who claimed to be a sorcerer heard of her gifts and suspected she wielded some kind of true magic he might steal. He traveled to Vasilka's tower, and at its base he met her father, tending to the garden. The sorcerer spoke not of Vasilka's talent or what fine tapestry he hoped to commission from her, but of his loneliness and his wish to just sit and talk awhile with this mysterious girl.

Vasilka's father had long since given up hope of anyone wishing to marry his strange and solitary daughter, and though her weaving kept them both well provided for, he wished that she might find a partner and have a family of her own. So he led the kindly seeming man up the winding stair and let him sit with Vasilka while she worked at her loom.

The sorcerer talked of the weather, of his travels, of what plays he had seen, an easy flow of conversation like the murmur of a brook, designed to lull Vasilka into giving up her secrets. Every so often, he would slip a real question into the gentle current of words.

"How is your thread more vibrant than any other weaver's?" he would ask.

"Do you think it's brighter?" Vasilka would reply, adding a skein of copper into the cloth she was working, its color so brilliant it seemed to burn itself into the pattern.

After a while, he'd try again. "How do you fashion the patterns of your cloth with such charm?"

"Do you find them charming?" was all Vasilka answered, finishing a neat row that might have been the silky edge of a feather.

The sorcerer hummed a bit, looked out one of the many windows. He filled Vasilka's glass with water, filled her ears with amusing gossip and tales of talking animals. Then he said, "Why do the colors of your tapestries never fade?"

"Don't they?" she asked, choosing a very sturdy bit of wool, so strong it might have borne any weight at all. "I never see them once they leave this room."

Every question the sorcerer asked, Vasilka would reply with a query of her own, until he grew frustrated and angry, his patience wearing away to nothing.

"Come live with me and be my bride," demanded the sorcerer at last. "I will teach you all the ways that you can use your gift and we will reign over every lesser creature. Refuse me and I will shove you from this tower. You can ask your foolish questions as you fall to your death."

But all the time the sorcerer had been talking, he had not bothered to understand just what Vasilka had been weaving—a grand pair of wings. All he could do was stare as she slipped them onto her arms and leapt from the tower. She soared away on golden feathers that caught the light in their glowing threads and seemed to set the last scraps of afternoon sun ablaze.

She is said to have become the first firebird and is the patron saint of unwed women.

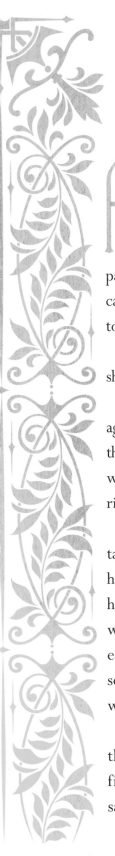

# SANKT NIKOLAI

A captain took his crew to sea, and because of his good leadership and the talent of his sailors, his ship came to be known as the fastest and most profitable on the ocean. It darted in and out of coves and ports, slipping past rocks and glaciers, a dancer on the waves. But the captain grew prideful and his crew greedy, and they began to ignore both sense and caution.

"What wind would dare cut down this ship?" the captain shouted to the sky.

A young boy was on the crew, a gifted sailor despite his age, who had learned to work the nets and lines and scaled the rigging fearlessly. He worried that the captain's pride would offend the Saints. But as it happened, the captain was right: It wasn't the wind that claimed his ship. It was the ice.

In the treacherous waters of the Bone Road, the captain piloted his sleek craft to pockets of fish no one else had dared seek so far north. Though it was late in the year, he insisted they could make one last run to fill their nets with cod before the winter set in. The ship made its way easily through the waters, the winds so favorable they seemed to serve the captain's whims. Later the sailors would wonder if the weather had been luring them north.

They put in at a cove with a black rock shore, and settled in for the night, prepared to haul up their catch at first light and then head home. But in the morning, the sailors woke to see the world had turned white. The sea had frozen around their ship, leaving them ice-locked. The winds blew, the sails filled, but the ship did not budge.

"Someone must scout the land to see if food or shelter can be found," said the captain. The crew knew that they were too far north to find aid, that to leave the ship was certainly folly and might very well mean death. So they sent the boy—the smallest and the youngest among them—out into the snow.

The boy's name was Nikolai, and he had always loved the sea and the Saints. Since the sea had stranded him, he hoped the Saints would protect him, and as he marched over the cold land, he sang his prayers like a shanty. Eventually he came to a high gray outcropping of rock that looked like a serpent asleep in the sun, though there was no sun to be seen. There, he found a reindeer waiting. Breath pluming in the air, the creature stomped its hooves and lowered its big head, and after a moment's hesitation, Nikolai climbed onto its back.

The beast carried him deep into a forest where the very trees seemed made of ice and the silver leaves on the silver branches tinkled like glasses clinking at a fine dinner party, and though the wind blew hard, Nikolai held tight to the reindeer's neck and felt only warm.

In time, they came to a clearing in the wood, and there the boy found a feast had been set beside a roaring fire. There was a small shelter and inside it, next to a high pile of thick blankets, Nikolai discovered a pair of fur-lined boots and a pair of woolen gloves. He put them on and found they fit perfectly.

Wishing to be polite, he waited to see if his host would appear. But time wore on, and his belly growled, and the only sound was the fire crackling and the reindeer snorting in the cold air.

Nikolai began by sipping from a hot ladle of spicy soup, rich with chunks of fish. He ate from a platter laden with juicy slices of roasted meat, buttery dumplings heaped with sour cream, stewed apples and candied plums that sparkled like fat amethysts. He drank warm wine and then, his belly full, fell deeply asleep.

The next morning, he made a sack from one of the blankets and packed it with all the leftover food he could manage. He climbed onto the reindeer's back and it carried him many miles to the serpent stone, where Nikolai dismounted, thanked the creature, and walked back to the ship.

The captain and the crew were shocked to see the little figure with the golden hair tramping toward them across the ice. They'd thought he must be dead, for who could survive the night in such a wilderness? As he drew nearer, they expected to find him hollow-eyed and ragged with hunger and cold. Instead his cheeks were pink, his stride even, his eyes bright.

The boy told them the wonderful story of what had happened in the night, but when he opened the sack to offer them food, all he found were rocks and ash. The sailors beat the boy for lying, took his fine gloves and boots for themselves, and the next morning, they shoved him back out onto the ice.

Again Nikolai walked to the serpent stone, and again, the reindeer was waiting. He rode the animal into the white forest and on to the clearing, where the fire crackled and a merry feast had been laid out once more. A red wool coat lined in lush fur lay neatly folded on the heap of blankets, another pair of boots, another pair of gloves. The boy did not know what to think of it, but the food was as real as he remembered. This time he ate goose glazed in honey and dressed in berries tart enough to sting his tongue as the juice ran down his chin. He bundled into the warm clothes and slept soundly through the night.

But when Nikolai returned to the ship the next day, the sack he carried was once more filled with rocks and ash. The crew beat him soundly and sent him onto the ice again.

It went on like this, and as time wore away, the men starved and the boy grew sturdier and stronger. With every day, the sailors' eyes grew wilder, and hunger became less a need than a madness. One morning, the sailors tried to follow Nikolai, but as soon as they spotted the serpent-shaped rock, a snowstorm overtook them. They wandered in circles all the day and night and returned to the ship even hungrier and angrier than before.

Soon an idea was whispered from one man to the next: What if they ate the boy? Who would know? He was fat and healthy, his cheeks rosy; he could feed them all for a week, maybe more, long enough for rescue to come or for the cold to break.

The boy heard these whispers and shivered in his bunk. As soon as dawn arrived, he raced out into the snow. This time when he met the reindeer, he whispered in its ear of all his fear and worry. But the reindeer had nothing to say.

Again, the boy sat by the fire, though he hadn't much appetite for the fine meal set out for him. He ate a bit of quail egg pie and a single sugared plum and prayed that the Saints would protect him, because he did not want to be eaten.

The next day, when the boy woke, he found he was sweating in his blankets. The sun beat heavy and hot on his neck as the reindeer carried him back to the serpent stone. And sure enough, as soon as he set foot upon the ship, the ice sighed and cracked. The boat rocked, the wind filled the sails, and the ship broke free.

At first, the sailors celebrated; all ill will vanished on the rising breeze. But as they drew closer to home, the men began to mutter to themselves, wondering what might happen if the boy told anyone how he had been treated aboard the ship and how his crewmates had nearly resorted to cannibalism. They began to think that perhaps the boy shouldn't reach home at all and soon set out to make sure he didn't. But every time they raised their knives, the winds would fall away, becalming the ship, its sails limp as wilted leaves. In this way, Nikolai survived the journey.

When the ship finally reached port, the sailors were met by disbelieving crowds. Their countrymen had assumed they had long since wrecked and perished. The crew praised their captain's ingenuity and said that everyone among them had banded together with courage and heart—all but the young boy Nikolai, who was not to be trusted, no matter what horrible tales he told. Nikolai said nothing but hurried to the first church he could find to offer prayers of thanks.

The captain and his crew were given medals and pronounced heroes. They were invited into the best homes and celebrated with feasts and parties. Tempted by mouthwatering smells and the sumptuous banquets laid out before them, again and again, they tried to eat. But none of them could manage much more than a bite. Every morsel of food tasted of stone and ash. One by one, they withered away and perished, desperate for just one spoonful of gravy, just one mouthful of wine.

As for Nikolai, he'd kept his fine red coat and the sack he'd used to try to bring food to the crew, and now each morning he woke to find the sack stuffed full of sweets and delicacies. So he took to traveling from village to village and house to house, laying feasts before the hungry, even when the world was at its coldest, even when the wind howled and snow lay thick on the ground.

He is known as the patron saint of sailors and lost causes, and it is traditional to set a place for him at the table on the darkest night of the year.

# SANKTA LIZABETA
# OF THE ROSES

There was a village, somewhere to the west, nestled in the shelter of a tall hill called Gorubun because of its crooked shape. From the top of this hill you could just see the blue promise of the ocean, and when the weather was right, the wind would carry the salt smell of the sea from the distant shore.

Every morning at dawn, the wise men of the village sent four scouts up the hill, and the four scouts would sit back to back, looking east, west, north, south to warn if any trouble might be headed their way. At dusk, four fresh scouts came to relieve them, and all through the night the new scouts sat, as the stars rose and black night bled away to morning again.

But the village was unremarkable, with nothing worth stealing, and attracted attention from neither thief nor marauder. And so, year after year, the scouts returned from the hill with little to report except pleasant breezes and stray sheep grazing outside their pastures.

Strong backs were needed to work the fields, and it seemed a waste to lose four good laborers each day and night, and so during one harvest, three of the scouts were permitted to remain down in the village and just one scout was sent to climb the crooked hill. When the harvest ended and there had been no trouble, the wise men of the village didn't so much decide not to reinstate the other scouts, as they forgot to order them up the hill again. One scout still climbed the slope every morning and another replaced him every night, and if one of them occasionally fell asleep or the other spent his hours kissing Marina Trevich, the stonemason's daughter, who was to know?

Lizabeta lived on the western outskirts of the village, far from the shadow of Gorubun. Each day she walked out to the meadows beyond her family's home to tend to their hives. She wore no gloves or bonnet. The bees let her take their honey without a single sting. There, where wild white roses grew in clouds of blossoms so profuse they looked like mist rolling in over the fields, Lizabeta would pray and think on the great works of the Saints, for even then she was a pious and serious girl. And there she was, the summer sun hot on her bent head, the bees humming lazily around her, when a breeze came from the west carrying not the salt-soaked tang of the sea but the smell of something burning.

Lizabeta ran home to tell her father. "It's probably nothing," he said. "The village due west is burning their trash. This is none of our concern."

But Lizabeta could not shake her unease, so she and her father walked to the neighboring manor house, the home of a prosperous and well-respected citizen. "Your father is right," he assured her. "It's probably nothing. Perhaps a roof caught fire. This is none of our concern."

And yet still, Lizabeta could not calm her restless thoughts, and so, to appease her, the merchant and her father accompanied her all the way into the village square to see the wise men, who gathered there beneath the red elm tree. Each day they would drink kvas, eat fresh bread brought to them by their wives, and puzzle over the great mysteries of the world.

When Lizabeta spoke of the scent of smoke blowing in over the meadow, the men said, "If there were any trouble, the scout atop Gorubun would give warning. Now leave us to think on the mysteries of the world."

All agreed with the wise men of the village. The merchant returned to his manor house, and Lizabeta's father took her home. But when Lizabeta sat and prayed among the hives, no peace came to her. So back through town she went and up the crooked hill; alone she climbed the narrow path. On the slopes of Gorubun, there was no stink of something burning, and the pastures seemed green and peaceful. She began to feel quite silly as her legs grew weary and sweat bloomed on her brow. Surely such concerns could be left to her father and the merchant and the wise men of the village.

Still she pressed on, between rocks and boulders, feeling more foolish with every step. When she reached the top of the hill, she found the scout snoring peacefully beneath his cap with his long legs stretched out on the soft grass. The air was fresh and clean, but when Lizabeta turned to the west, she saw a terrible thing: columns of smoke like dark pillars holding up a heavy sky. And she knew that it was not just refuse she'd smelled burning or a kitchen fire. She'd caught the scent of churches set alight and bodies too.

She ran back down the hill, fast as she could without falling, and into the town square.

"An army!" Lizabeta cried. "An army is marching!" She told them she'd seen pillars of fire, one for each town between their village and the sea. "We must gather swords and arrows and go to our neighbors' aid!"

"We will discuss it," said the wise men of the village. "We will raise a defense."

But when Lizabeta had gone, and they were no longer faced with the pleas of a frightened girl, the idea of a war seemed far less heroic. The wise men had all been children the last time fighting had come to the village. They had no desire to pick up blades and shields. They did not want to see their sons do that either.

"Surely the soldiers will pass us by, as they always have before," the wise men told themselves. And they went to have dinner and to ponder the great mysteries of the world.

When dawn came, Lizabeta went out to the meadow to wait for the brave men of the village to arrive with their swords and shields. She waited as the sun drifted higher and the bees hummed around her. She waited as the roses wilted beneath the heat, their white petals browning at the edges. No one came. Until, at last, she heard marching footsteps, not from the direction of the village, but from the darkness of the woods. She heard voices raised in battle song and felt thunder through the earth. She understood then that there would be no rescue.

But Lizabeta did not turn to run. When the men appeared, ferocious and covered in blood and soot and sweat, mad with the taking of lives and treasure, Lizabeta knelt amid the roses. "Mercy," she pleaded. "Mercy for my father, for the merchant, for the wise men who cower in their houses. Mercy for me."

The men were mad with bloodlust and triumph. They roared as they rushed the clearing, and if they heard Lizabeta's pleas, their steps did not waver. She was a sapling before them to bend and be trampled. She was a river that must part. She was nothing and no one, a girl on her knees with prayers on her lips, full of terror, full of rage. From the hives surrounding the clearing came a low, thrumming note, a song that rose, vibrating through the air. The bees emerged in dense, whirring clouds, like smoke from a village set ablaze, swarming over the soldiers, swaddling them in crawling bodies, and the men began to scream.

The soldiers turned their backs on Lizabeta and her tiny army, and ran.

If only this were where the story ended, Lizabeta would be made a hero, a statue of her raised in the town square, and the wise men would meet beneath it each day to remind themselves of their own cowardice and to be humbled in the shadow of a girl.

But none of these things came to pass. Word spread, of course, that the raiders had come to the coast and marched inland. But no one outside the village knew why they'd suddenly changed their course and fled back to the sea. There were rumors of some fantastical weapon, others of a terrible plague or a curse brought down by a witch.

Word of the town that had been mysteriously spared reached a general who was assembling a great army to face the raiders when they returned. With a few of his best men, he marched to the village where the enemy had ceased their invasion. He went to the wise men who met in the town square, and when he asked them how they had turned the tide of battle and sent such fearsome enemies running, they looked to one another, afraid of what the general might do if they told him silly stories of girls and bees. "Well, we cannot say," the wise men offered. "But we know a merchant who can."

When the general reached the manor house, the merchant said, "It is difficult to explain, but the beekeeper down the road will know."

And when at last the general came to Lizabeta's home and knocked on the door, her father saw the fearsome men with their armor and their hard faces and he trembled. "I cannot be certain what happened," he told them. "But surely my daughter will know. She is in the meadow, tending to her hives."

Lizabeta met them there. "What made the enemy turn in their tracks?" demanded the general of the girl in the meadow. "What made them flee this nothing of a village?"

Lizabeta told the truth. "Only the bees know."

Now, the general was tired and angry and had walked many miles only to be taunted by a young girl. He was out of patience. His men bound Lizabeta's wrists and her ankles and placed the ropes over the bridles of four strong horses. Again, he asked Lizabeta how she had stopped the soldiers.

"Only the bees know," she whispered. For she hadn't any idea how she'd done it or what miracle had transpired.

The general waited, certain that the girl's father or the merchant or the wise men of the village would come to her aid and tell him their secrets.

"Do not bother waiting," she said. "No one is coming."

So the general gave the order, as generals do, and Lizabeta's body was torn apart, and the bees hummed lazily in their hives. It's said her blood watered the roses of the field and turned the blossoms red. It's said the blooms planted on her grave never perished and smelled sweet the whole year round, even when the winter snows came. But the bees have long since left those hives and want no business with those flowers.

If you can find that meadow, you may stand and breathe in the perfume of its blossoms, speak your prayers, and let the wind carry them west to the sea.

The roses remember, even if wise men choose to forget.

Lizabeta is known as the patron saint of gardeners.

# SANKTA
# MARADI

I n a great bay on the coast of Novyi Zem, two families had fished for many generations, and had squabbled over the rights to those waters for just as long. Addis Endewe and Neda Adaba could scarcely speak a civil word to each other. As their competing fleets grew, so did their profits—and so did the enmity between them. The fishermen in their employ were known to cut each other's nets, tear holes in their rivals' sails, and pull their boats alongside so that the crews could better punch and kick each other.

But then, as is the way of these things, on a market day, Addis Endewe's son, Duli, went with his friends to buy jurda at the very same time that Neda Adaba's daughter, Baya, had a craving for sweet oranges. There, amid the fruit stalls and shouting fishmongers, Duli and Baya fell immediately in love. Perhaps, if their families hadn't hated one another, it would have been a passing infatuation and nothing more. Or perhaps they would have fallen in love anyway. Maybe some people are destined for one another and lucky enough to know it when they finally meet.

Handsome Duli and beautiful Baya began meeting in secret on the property of Sankta Maradi, who lived near the shore. When people left the old woman gifts, the skies had a way of clearing and lost ships somehow found their way to harbor. She let the lovers meet on her little dock, where they mended nets together, and watched the stars, and hatched a plan to run away. They agreed they would each steal a boat from their family fleets and meet beyond the bay, where their parents' rivalry could not touch them.

Duli crept out after dark, secured a small skiff, and sailed off beneath a cloudy and starless sky. But Baya's father caught her trying to escape, and in his rage, had his entire fleet smashed to splinters rather than see his daughter wed to his enemy's son.

Baya would not be deterred. Despite the darkness, she leapt into the sea, her limbs fighting the pull of the current as she struggled through the waves, calling out to Duli.

Their names echoed across the bay as they tried to find their way to each other, but the sea was cold and the clouds hung heavy, blocking the light of the moon. From her lonely pier Sankta Maradi heard them calling back and forth, back and forth in the darkness. She took pity on the lovers who wished for a new world together instead of an old world divided. With a single gesture from Maradi, the clouds parted and the moon emerged, gilding the world in silver light.

Duli and Baya found each other across the glimmering waves. Duli pulled his love up into the boat and they sailed to safety, far away from their families. They began a new life, on a new shore, and chose a new family name: Maradi, and this is where the Zemeni tradition of choosing names began.

Every year, the Maradi family made a path of white stones, each one round as the moon, down to the water, where they said prayers of thanks for the life they'd been able to make together.

Sankta Maradi is known as the patron saint of impossible love.

# SANKT DEMYAN
# OF THE RIME

In the icy eastern reaches of Fjerda, a cemetery stood, and among its rows were both humble graves marked by nothing but wooden staves, and fine mausoleums hewn of marble, grand houses for the dead.

A forest grew up around this cemetery, and at first the people paid the trees no mind, happy for their shade. But soon the birches grew so thick and so dense that no one could reach the cemetery to tend to the graves of their family members or pay homage to their ancestors.

They went to Demyan, the nobleman whose land the forest had grown upon, and asked that he do something about the trees. Demyan had his servants go out to the forest with their axes and cut a smooth path to the cemetery so that all could walk comfortably through the woods.

But when the rains came, without trees to stop the floods, water rushed straight down the path to the graveyard, uprooting markers and gravestones and casting the lids off tombs.

Again, the townspeople came to complain. This time, Demyan designed an aqueduct and had it built around the cemetery so that the rain would not disturb the graves and the water would be diverted to irrigate the fields. But the aqueduct cast the graveyard in shade, so plants and flowers rarely grew there, and now families shivered in the cold when they went to visit their dead.

Yet again the people brought their grievances to

Demyan. But this time he was not certain what to do. He walked the path to the cemetery through the woods and looked up at the tall aqueduct and laid his hands upon the soil. He could think of no solution that would make his people happy, unless the Saints saw fit to raise the cemetery up to the sun itself.

The earth began to shake and the ground rose high, higher, a mountain where there had been no mountain before. When the rumbling stopped, the cemetery perched at its top, where it would never be troubled by floods or crowded by trees.

The people followed Demyan up to the cemetery and found that no grave had been disturbed or soul displaced. Only one tomb was cracked: Demyan's family crypt.

Maybe they were shaken by the wonders they had seen. Maybe they did not know how to be satisfied. Whatever the reason, the people Demyan had sought so hard to please threw up their hands in woe. They claimed that he had disrespected his family name. They cried that he had cursed them all by using dark magic. Someone picked up a piece of marble from the broken tomb and hurled it at Demyan. Driven mad by getting what they wanted, the others followed, hurling stones at the nobleman until he lay crumpled beneath the ruins of his own family crypt.

It is said that the tallest mountain in the Elbjen is the one upon which Demyan died. He is known as the patron saint of the newly dead.

# SANKTA MARYA
# OF THE ROCK

I n the summers, a gathering of Suli often traveled south to Ravka's border. They would work until the weather began to turn cold, then they would pack up and travel over the Sikurzoi and into the warmer territories of Shu Han. In some places they were turned away by townspeople who refused them any spot to camp. In others, people hostile to the Suli would descend upon their settlements at night with torches and hounds.

But there were some places where the Suli were welcome. Where Suli knowledge was respected, they were offered bread and wine, and pasture for their animals. Where amusement was wanted, the Suli were free to erect their tents and perform their entertainments to happy applause. And where there was work to be done— grimy work, dangerous work that no one else wanted or dared to take on—the Suli were welcomed in those places as well.

The horse races at Caryeva usually lasted late into the fall, and so the Suli often spent the season there. But one year, winter came early, closing down the track and leaving them without work or audiences to play for. A local offered the men jobs in his copper mine, and though the prospect was risky and the Suli knew many had died in the mine's dark tunnels, they agreed.

However, the night before the men were meant to

enter the pits, one of the Suli true seers looked into the leavings of her coffee and warned them not to go into the tunnels. She was known for the clarity of her vision, and none of them took her words lightly.

"What can we do to save ourselves?" they asked.

The old woman placed the jackal mask of the Suli seers over her face and sat for a long time as the others talked quietly by the fire. When the moon had set and the fire had burned down to nothing but ash, she lifted one gnarled hand and pointed to a little girl. "Marya must go with you."

No one liked this idea, not the girl's parents, and least of all Marya herself, who still feared the dark. But the next day, when the men set out for the mines, she summoned her courage, took her rag doll in her arms, and clambered onto her father's shoulders. Into the pits they went, the rock walls close around them, the air moist, the smell of copper in the earth like spilled blood.

The morning passed without incident, then the afternoon, and then the day was done. The workers heaved a sigh of relief and turned to make their way out of the tunnel, back to sunlight and the living world.

That was when the earth began to rumble. The tunnel ahead of them collapsed, blocking out all daylight. But just as the ceiling was about to give way above their heads, Marya, still clutching her rag doll, lifted her little hands. The ceiling held.

The rock walls of the mine shifted like silt in a pan. They shuddered and slid, making an opening so that the Suli might pass. Through the mountain they went, led by Marya on her father's shoulders, the rock giving way to form a path before them.

They emerged on the other side and there, at the base of the Sikurzoi, the Suli have always been able to find shelter in the caves that Marya left behind.

She is known as the patron saint of those who are far from home.

# SANKT EMERENS

The village of Girecht in southern Kerch had long been known for the purity and flavor of its grain, as well as the perfection of the beer made from its barley and hops. Each year when the leaves began to turn, the townspeople set long tables in the main square, hung the trees with lanterns, and welcomed guests from all over Kerch to fill their bellies with the town's beer and fill Girecht's coffers with their coin.

The next day, they would go to church to give thanks to Ghezen and their Saints. But one year, the townspeople had grown too merry in their celebrations, and the morning after the festival, they lay abed with headaches instead of going to pray. All but one child, a young boy named Emerens.

Now this child had been pious since his birth. He never cried on Saints' days—except when the townspeople were late to services. Then he would bawl and howl, his shrill wail carrying over the rooftops and through every window, and nothing might soothe him until his parents and their neighbors went to church. On the morning after that very merry festival, Emerens knocked on every door, trying to rouse the citizens of Girecht, but all refused to answer.

Who can say if what came to pass next was merely bad luck or the hand of providence? Either way, a blight struck Girecht's fields the following year, leaving the grain spotted and dying.

The villagers managed to cull enough untainted grain to fill four silos, enough for two years' worth of festivals. They hung lanterns in the main square and set out long tables for feasting. But the next morning, they found that the western silo was a quarter empty. A search revealed ragged holes in the silo's sides, where some of the grain had spilled out. One of the farmers climbed to the top of the silo, opened the hatch, and shrieked his horror, for the structure was full of rats, their hairy bodies and pink tails thrashing about as they gorged themselves.

The next day the eastern silo was found to have been infested, and the townspeople knew that the northern and southern silos would follow.

"What can we do?" they cried. "If we poison the rats, we'll poison the grain and we will have no way to make beer for our festival."

Young Emerens had the answer. "Lower me into the eastern silo and I will chase the rats away."

The townspeople were disgusted by such a notion, but since they did not have to go swimming about with vermin themselves, they were willing to try it. They tied a rope around Emerens' waist and lowered him into the grain like a bucket being dropped down a well.

Sure enough, as soon as Emerens sank into the grain, the rats sensed his holiness and chewed their way clear, eager to be away from such goodness. It took many hours of Emerens being lifted and dunked into the grain, but soon all the rats were gone and the grain was pure again.

The citizens of Girecht pronounced Emerens the savior of the village, hefted him up on their shoulders, and carried him around the town square, cheering his good name.

The next day, when the festival was to begin, the townspeople saw that, just as they had predicted, the rats had infested the southern silo. In went Emerens and the rats began to flee.

It was a long process, and as the evening wore on, the villagers minding Emerens' rope heard music coming from the town square, heard the thump of people dancing, and smelled the syrups and sweet cakes and sausages they knew were being piled high onto platters just a short distance away. Surely, they thought, we can race down to the square, have a dance and a drink, and be back before we need to pull up the boy.

The next time Emerens sank into the silo, they raced down to the square. But after the first sip of beer, they couldn't help but take a second. One dance became two and then three as the fiddles swelled around them, and soon they forgot that they'd ever been meant to do anything that night but enjoy themselves.

In the darkness of the silo, Emerens tugged on the rope in vain, waiting to be drawn up to the surface. There he died, floating in the grain, his mouth and eyes and nose full of barley. The next day, the townspeople slept soundly in their beds, long after the bells for morning services had rung. Only late in the afternoon, when they stumbled to their kitchen tables and threw their shutters open to the sunlight, did anyone wonder why Emerens had not come to call them to prayer.

Emerens was buried in the barley fields, but since his death, beer or bread made from Girecht grain has forever tasted of misery, and leaves anyone who consumes it with a sour stomach and melancholy thoughts.

Girecht and its bitter fields are long forgotten, but Emerens, patron saint of brewers, is paid homage in late summer when the harvest begins.

# SANKT VLADIMIR
# THE FOOLISH

I f you are lucky, you may have stood on the quay in the great city of Os Kervo and gazed in awe at its famous lighthouse and the massive seawall that protects it. Neither would have ever come to be without the work of a brave boy named Vladimir.

The bay at Os Kervo was once an untamed place where the sea savaged the shore and tossed ships against the land like bits of driftwood. For long years the people who had settled there tried to make the bay a working port. But all their efforts to build piers and protections were nothing against the fury of the ocean.

It seemed a hopeless cause, so when it was announced that the king would seek to land a fleet of ships on their shores, the people did not know what to do. This was their chance at prosperity, to be recognized by the king, whose attention might forever change their fortunes. Yet if the king could not land, it would all be for nothing and some other, gentler harbor would gain their ruler's favor.

Vladimir was a young man without talents. He was not strong enough to be of help with building or farming or heavy work; neither was he particularly clever or interesting. He could not sing well and he was not pleasing to look at. Vladimir knew all this and the knowledge made him halting and shy, which only seemed to bother people more. They would call him "fool" or shoo him from their door, and Vladimir found that he was loneliest around other people. He was happier wandering down to the edge of the water to whisper to the waves.

Still, Vladimir listened closely to the conversations that eddied around him. He heard his neighbors worry and argue over the arrival of the king's fleet, and he thought he might know a solution. But when he opened his mouth to speak, his words washed away and he was left to endure blank stares and exasperated sighs. The easiest thing would be to do what he must alone.

Vladimir waded into the water up to his knees, and then up to his hips, and then up to his chest. At first the people jeered and shouted. Until they saw that the water was going with him, the tide receding as he walked farther and farther from the land. The waves trailed him, the ocean pulling away from shore like a woman gathering her skirts. The people of the bay saw the extraordinary chance he'd given them and took up their hammers and chisels.

For thirty days and thirty nights, Vladimir stood in the water and held back the sea, whispering his prayers as the sun rose and fell, and crabs nibbled at his toes, until the great seawall and the base of the lighthouse were built.

At last, the foreman signaled to Vladimir that the work was done and he could finally rest. But Vladimir was too tired to make the walk back to land. He lowered his hands, his prayers fell silent, and the wild sea rushed in.

Vladimir's body drifted to shore on the tide, and the people of Os Kervo gathered him up and placed him upon a bier covered in lilies. For another thirty days and thirty nights, they came to pay their respects, and to the astonishment of all, Vladimir's corpse did not rot. On the thirty-first day, his body dissolved into sea-foam, leaving behind nothing but a small heap of sea salt among the lilies.

He is known as the patron saint of the drowned and of unlikely achievement.

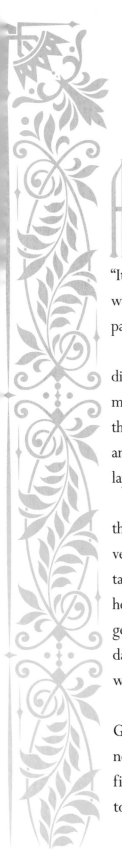

# SANKT GRIGORI
# OF THE WOOD

A nobleman's son fell ill with a disease that none of his father's wise friends and advisers had ever seen before.

"He must be bled," decreed the local physician who had served the nobleman's household for many years. "It is the only thing for such cases." So the young man's veins were opened and leeches were applied, but he only grew paler and weaker in his bed.

"He must be made warm," declared the mayor, who dined at the nobleman's house every week. "Such diseases must be sweated out." So they swaddled the young man in thick blankets and kept a fire blazing in the hearth all day and night. Sure enough, he sweated through all his many layers of bedclothes, but he grew no stronger.

"He must be left to rest in the dark like a root," said the nobleman's rich neighbor, who was known for his prize vegetables. "A long sleep will restore him." Heavy black curtains were drawn over the windows, and the young man's head was wrapped in thick cotton batting so no sound could get through. When the door to his room was opened three days later, he did look white and lifeless as a turnip, but he was no better.

At last, the nobleman's wife took charge and sent for Grigori, a healer and teacher who lived in the mountains nearby. It took many days for the nobleman's emissaries to find the healer's cave, but when at last they did, he agreed to follow them down the mountain.

Grigori was distressed when he saw the state of the nobleman's home. He opened the windows and let in the fresh air. He banked the fire and tossed the leeches onto the coals. What else he did is not known, but only a few days later, the young man sat up in bed and declared that he was hungry. The next day he rose and walked with his mother around the garden. And the day after that, he asked that his horse be brought to him so that he might go for a ride.

The nobleman showered Grigori with praise, and a great feast was held in his honor. But the physician, and the mayor, and the rich neighbor were not pleased by this turn of events. They had all long benefited from the nobleman's favor, and they did not like to see him turning to a new adviser.

They began to whisper in the nobleman's ear, tales of bizarre doings in the mountains. They claimed Grigori played with dark magic and that he had used that very magic to heal the nobleman's son. They brought forth witnesses who said they had seen Grigori talking to beasts and making corpses dance for his amusement. Though his son and his wife pleaded for mercy, the nobleman could not ignore such terrible charges and had Grigori taken to the wood and left there overnight to be devoured by beasts.

As dusk fell and the creatures of the wood began to howl, Grigori was afraid, but he whispered to his Saints for guidance. When he knelt to pray, he saw that, at his feet, were the bones of others who had been brought to the wood to face a death sentence. From those bones, he fashioned a lyre, and when the animals drew near, he played a sad and haunting tune that rose from his fingertips and up into the branches, the melody hanging in the air like mist. The wolves ceased their slavering and laid their heads upon their paws. The snakes hissed contentedly, lying still as if upon a sun-warmed rock. The bears curled up and dreamed of when they were cubs and all they knew was their mothers' milk, the rush of the river, and the smell of wildflowers.

In the morning, the soldiers returned and when they found Grigori alive and well, the nobleman's son declared, "You see? This must mean that he is holy."

But the physician, and the mayor, and the rich neighbor all said it was yet another sign that Grigori trafficked in dark magic, and that if he was allowed to live, the nobleman and his family would most certainly be cursed.

Grigori was taken to the wood once more, and this time his hands were bound. Night fell, and the creatures of the wood howled, and unable to play his lyre, Grigori was torn apart by the very beasts who had slept so peacefully at his feet the night before.

He is known as the patron saint of doctors and musicians.

# SANKT
# VALENTIN

ust days before her wedding was to take place, a young
bride fell ill, and though she fought valiantly and was
tended to with love and care and many prayers, she
perished. These were the worst days of winter, and
because the ground was too cold to give way to shovels
or picks, no proper grave could be dug. The girl's family
was too poor to afford a mausoleum. So they dressed
the girl in the silks that would have been her bridal gown
and laid her down upon a slab in the icehouse, her hands
folded over her breast, her fingers clutching a bouquet of
leaves and winter berries. Each day, her family would sit
awhile and visit with her, and the young man who should
have been her groom came to weep over the body long
into the night.

When the first thaw arrived, a grave was dug on hallowed ground and the girl was lowered into it, a plain
headstone marking her place of rest.

But the next morning, when the girl's mother went to
visit her daughter's grave, she found a snake curled upon the
headstone, its scales gleaming black in the sun. The woman
stood shaking, fresh flowers in her hands, too afraid to
approach, until finally, tears on her cheeks, she gave up and
returned home.

All spring, the grieving woman would visit the cemetery with a new bouquet in hand. The snake would lift its
flat head at her approach and sometimes slither down the

stone to the gently mounded dirt. But it never left the girl's grave and so no one could come to pay their respects—not her mother, not her father, not the heartbroken young man who had loved her.

The woman went to the church and prayed to Sankt Valentin, the patron saint of snake charmers and the lonely, and that night, Sankt Valentin spoke to her.

"Go to the grave," he said, "lie down on the ground beside the snake, and all will be revealed to you."

The woman trembled. "I cannot!" she pleaded. "I am too afraid."

But Sankt Valentin's voice was steady. "You can choose faith or you can choose fear. But only one will bring what you long for."

So the next day, the woman walked to the cemetery, and when she saw the snake lying in the new green grass that had sprung up over her daughter's grave, she didn't turn away, but still shaking, made herself lie down on the damp earth. The serpent lifted its head, its glittering eyes like mourning beads. Certain it was about to strike, the woman prepared to feel the snake's bite and join her daughter in the next life.

But instead, the serpent spoke, its slender tongue tasting the air.

"Mama," it said, "it is I, the spirit of your lost daughter, returned to tell you of my plight. I did not die of natural illness, but from poison, fed to me in what was meant to be medicine by the man who swore he loved me until I told him I did not love him any longer and did not wish to be his bride. He laughed over my corpse in the icehouse, and now he is afraid to visit this grave, for he knows the Saints will not allow a murderer to feign honest prayer on hallowed ground."

The woman wept, and let the snake curl gently around her wrist, and told her daughter she loved her. Then she marched down to the town and found the man who had claimed to love her daughter.

"You must go with me to the cemetery," she said, "and pay your final respects to my daughter, who would have been your bride and whom you swore to love."

The young man protested. Hadn't he already visited her countless nights in the cold of the icehouse? And wasn't there a snake said to be lurking around the headstones?

"What righteous man fears a snake?" she demanded. "What man professes love, then will not speak his prayers on hallowed ground?"

The townspeople agreed and wondered why the young man resisted. At last, he submitted and followed her to the cemetery. When his footsteps slowed, she seized his hand and dragged him along the path. They passed through the gates and on to the girl's grave, where the snake lay curled upon it.

"Go on," said the woman. "Kneel and speak your prayers."

As soon as the young man opened his mouth, the snake uncoiled and sprang up, biting him right on the tongue. He died with the black tongue of a murderer, and was buried in unconsecrated ground, and was mourned by no one.

The snake was never seen again, but a quince tree grew beside the young bride's grave and lovers often met beneath its branches, when the weather was warm enough.

It is customary for the mothers of brides to offer prayers to Sankt Valentin, and seeing a snake on your wedding day is known to be good luck.

# SANKT PETYR

nstead of going to services on his Saint's day, a boy in the village of Brevno chose to sneak away with a jug of his father's cider and lay down to snore in the chicken yard.

While he slept, a demon crept into his mouth and slid down his throat, and when he woke he was not the same boy he had been. He bit his mother's cheek and set fire to the village school. He gnashed his teeth and tore up the prayer books in the chapel. When at last the boy fell asleep in his bed, a priest was called to speak holy words over his dreaming body and drive the demon out.

The thing that emerged from the boy's mouth was wet and gray as a slug, and though it thrashed and howled, it eventually let go its hold on the boy's insides. But the priest had failed to seal the house shut and the demon fled through an open window.

As you know, demons are drawn to water, and the creature took up residence in a nearby lake. Anytime someone approached the water to fish or take a drink, the demon would emerge, hiding its true form to entice its victim. Sometimes it appeared as a siren with smooth skin and damp lips who sang to young men of love. Sometimes it was a lost mother crooning a lullaby, or an old friend bellowing a happy drinking song. The demon always found the right melody to draw its prey closer, and as soon as the hunter or farmer or widow or child dipped their fingers into the water, the demon would seize that hopeless person by the wrist and drag its victim down to the smooth stones at the lake's bottom. There it would finish its song, as the cold seeped into its prey's bones and water filled the lungs of another poor lost soul. Only then would the demon release the body and let it float to shore.

The townspeople knew that nothing could destroy the demon but fire. The men of Brevno filled their quivers with burning arrows, but the monster was too canny to ever stray out of the lake. Whenever the hunters got close enough to the shore to take aim, the demon would begin to sing and coax them down beneath the surface.

The priest who had let the demon escape his grasp had long since vanished from the town in shame. But the young priest who came to replace him was a different kind of man. Petyr had the strength of the Saints and he was not afraid to approach the lake. He told the men to gather their arrows, dip them in pitch, and be ready.

He marched down to the water, and as he drew closer, he began to recite the *Sikurian Psalms*. When he was only a few feet away he saw his brother before him, singing the filthy old shanty they'd learned from their father, a song they'd laughed over together for hours as children. But of course, his brother had been crushed by the wheel of a horse cart before he'd reached his twentieth year. Petyr was not deceived. He spoke the psalms louder, shouting them, drowning out the voice of the demon.

Petyr stood on the rocks and leaned out over the lake so the demon would see his face and be tempted to emerge to claim him. He chanted as it sang, but he made his expression rapt, pretending to be lured. He reached his hand out as if to touch the water. Then just as his fingers were about to break the surface, Petyr drew back, and the demon shrieked in frustration.

He did this again and again, drawing back a little bit farther each time, until at last, the demon lifted its slippery head out of the water and climbed over the rocks toward him. The demon stretched its limbs, yearning toward Petyr, about to seize him.

The hunters let their arrows fly.

The demon tried to flee, but Petyr grabbed it by the wrist and held it tight. Fiery arrows rained down upon them both.

Though his cloak caught fire and his chest was pierced again and again, Petyr would not let go. He died that day, but so did the demon. The lake was freed and the villagers could frequent its shores without fear, though its waters always felt colder than they had before.

Sankt Petyr is known as the patron saint of archers.

# SANKTA YERYIN
# OF THE MILL

In the Shu capital of Ahmrat Jen, the palaces of noble families line the boulevards, grander and more elegant than any city in the world. Every spring, these nobles throw open the doors of their homes to their wealthy neighbors, festoon the pathways with peonies and apricot blossoms, and compete with one another to see who can serve the most delicious and elaborately decorated custard cakes.

Long ago, a nobleman invited friends from far and wide to celebrate with him. He intended to host a decadent banquet, imagining table after table laid with sweet fried cakes. But when he went to his storehouses, he found that the shelves were nearly empty and only one bag of flour remained, barely enough to make dough for a dozen guests.

The nobleman cursed and called for his miller. But the miller reminded him that over the year, the nobleman had given away all his flour to his rich friends in an attempt to impress them. Though there was plenty of wheat, there was no way to grind it into flour in time for the party.

In a rage, the nobleman denied this and accused his miller of being a thief. The miller's daughter, Yeryin, begged him to spare her father's life and promised that the next day, if the Saints were kind, the storehouse would be full of finely milled flour. Though the nobleman agreed to stay the miller's execution, he locked Yeryin inside the mill and posted his soldiers outside, for he suspected the girl was as dishonest as her father.

At dawn the next morning, the nobleman arrived with his many finely dressed friends. If he could not offer them a feast, he would at least provide them the spectacle of a hanging. But when he opened the doors to the storehouse, he saw flour bags stacked to the ceiling and a very tired Yeryin snoozing on the floor.

The nobleman kicked her with his boot. "Where did you get all this flour? You could not have ground it all in a single night."

"The Saints made me able," said Yeryin.

"Surely it will be coarse and unusable," he declared. But each bag was full of the finest, whitest flour ever seen.

You would think that the nobleman would have been happy, but he was convinced that Yeryin and her father had somehow managed to steal the flour and make a fool of him. Since his soldiers claimed Yeryin had never left the mill, he concluded that she must have dug a tunnel. He sent for shovels and picks and a cask of wine and he and his friends tore up the ground, making a merry game of it. They dug so deep and so far that eventually, no one could hear their voices or the sound of their pickaxes.

The miller opened the storehouses and invited all his and his daughter's friends to help themselves to flour. Then the servants of the vanished nobles sat down to a great feast and toasted Yeryin many times over.

She is the patron saint of hospitality.

# SANKT FELIKS
# AMONG THE BOUGHS

hen Ravka was still a young country, less a nation than a squabbling band of noblemen and soldiers unified beneath the young King Yarowmir's banner, a terrible winter came. It was not that this winter was any colder than those before it, only that spring did not arrive when it was meant to. The clouds did not part to let the sun warm the tree branches and turn them green. No thaw came to melt the snow. Throughout the countryside, pastures remained barren and frozen.

Yet in the Tula Valley, beneath a hard gray sky, the orchards somehow bloomed. Those trees were cared for by a man named Feliks, said to be a warrior monk who had once taken the shape of a hawk to fight for King Yarowmir. Each night, the people of the valley claimed they saw visions near the orchards. Some saw a red sun that floated overhead, some a wall of burning thorns, others a black horse with a mane of fire and hooves that sparked when they struck the ground, igniting rivers of blue flame.

In the mornings, they would argue about what they'd seen, each tale taller than the last. All they knew for certain was that the orchards did not succumb to frost. New flowers sprouted on the trees, blossoms white as stars that turned pink, then red, then vanished as the boughs filled with hard green nubs of new fruit.

As the cold sat stubborn over the rest of Ravka, the Tula Valley flourished, and eventually, those who suffered without a harvest grew jealous of the valley's bounty. They came with torches and swords to accuse Feliks of witchcraft, despite his reputation as a holy man.

The people of the valley had been well fed throughout the cold months. Their limbs were strong, their children healthy, their livestock sturdy. When they saw the light from the torches, they could have banded together to protect Feliks. Instead, they huddled in their homes, their gratitude withered by terror as a bud is withered by frost. They feared the mob would turn on them and did not want to lose all they had, even if that meant forgetting the man who had given it to them. So they let the outsiders put Feliks to the pyre.

The mob skewered Feliks on the slender, thorny trunk of a young apple tree and hung him like a side of mutton over a bed of hot coals, demanding that he confess to being a practitioner of dark magic.

Feliks told them there was no magic, only nature. He refused to confess to any crime and only asked to be turned on the spit so as to cook more evenly. His bones were scattered over the ground, and without his care, the orchards froze and faltered. Ever after, the only tree that would grow in that soil was the thorn wood, its branches thick with fruit that never ripened. The people of the Tula Valley starved along with everyone else and had their equal share of misery.

Sankt Feliks is celebrated in the spring with feasts of quince and apple and is known as the patron saint of horticulture.

# SANKT LUKIN
# THE LOGICAL

nce there was a prince who desperately wanted to be a king. He had among his councilors a wise man named Lukin, who could always be counted upon for sage advice and plenty of it. There were those who said that Lukin talked too much, others who likened him to a prattling bird, and still others who were known to discreetly place cotton in their ears when Lukin cleared his throat to speak.

While it was true Lukin's speeches were so long that young men grew beards and wheat came to harvest in the time it took him to reach his point, that point was most often sound. He predicted how many soldiers a rival prince would have waiting and when he meant to attack; he foresaw a year of drought and wisely admonished the prince to set aside stores of water; he guided the prince to prudent investment in merchant expeditions that brought back chests full of jewels and gold.

Once, when a neighboring army was threatening to invade, the prince sent Lukin to negotiate with them. When it came time for Lukin to plead his case, he spoke—and kept speaking, one argument leading to the next and then the next, in an endless tide of words. Soon the general nodded off and then his colonels, and then the sergeants and so on, until every last member of the invading army had been bored first to sleep and then to death.

The prince rewarded Lukin's bloodless victory and continued to heed his advice. In time, just as the prince had dreamed, and Lukin had predicted, he became king.

With Lukin's help the new king ruled successfully, expanding his territory and his power. But life was not without its troubles. The king's first wife vanished in the night with a swineherd, leaving nothing but a note behind confessing that she would rather tend pigs if wearing a crown meant listening to Lukin talk. His second wife joined a troupe of traveling circus performers. His third wife ate a bad oyster and died, but no one was certain if it was truly an accident. Each of these women gave the king a son.

As the king grew older, he worried that his death would bring chaos for the kingdom if each of his sons vied for the throne. He knew he had to choose an heir, so as he always did, he went to Lukin for advice.

After many hours of holding forth on the various factors and possible outcomes each choice might imply, Lukin did something he rarely did—he paused.

This resulted in the king doing something he'd never had reason to do before—he urged Lukin to go on.

Lukin confessed that the king had sired three fools, each son more incautious and venal than the last. None of them were fit to rule and all would bring great misery to the land.

"Well," said the king, "if you cannot tell me who will make the best king, perhaps you can tell me who would make the least terrible king."

After much debate, during which the moon rose and fell and rose again, Lukin pronounced that the second son might possibly—under the proper conditions, with all due allowances for temperament, and given appropriate and judicious counsel—make the least disastrous ruler.

The king called the court together, and before all his retainers, he decreed that upon his death, the throne would pass to his second son—on one condition. His son must vow to keep Lukin, the king's oldest, wisest adviser, beside him, to offer sage counsel until the end of Lukin's days. Before all the court, the second son gave his word, and a few years later, when his father passed, he was crowned with all due ceremony.

His first act as king was to call for Lukin's execution. As eager as many of the old king's retainers were for a bit of respite from Lukin's tongue, they had heard the second son give his solemn word. Such a vow could not be broken.

"Ah," said the second son, "but all I promised was to keep Lukin as my adviser until the end of his days. That end will simply come sooner than predicted."

The courtiers agreed that this did meet the letter of the vow, and some even marveled at the new king's cleverness. Perhaps he wouldn't need an adviser after all.

Lukin was marched to the executioner's block and went to his knees with prayers on his lips, for even in these moments before his own death, he had no use for silence. The executioner raised his axe and with a single clean slice cut Lukin's head from his body. There was a *thunk* as it landed and rolled onto its side, and though the gathered courtiers knew they must not cheer a wise man's death, they did heave a great sigh at the sudden, glorious quiet, broken by no dire predictions of disasters to come, nor instructions for the best way to prepare venison, nor disquisitions on the great earthquake of Vandelor.

A bird chirped outside the window. In some distant corner of the castle, a woman laughed. The young king smiled.

Then a voice broke the silence.

Lukin's head lay in the dust, but his eyes were still open and his lips had begun to move again. Having one's head removed from one's body was a most novel experience and brought to mind a great many lessons, which he was most delighted to share.

The second son was forced to honor his vow or lose his crown. Lukin's head was placed upon a golden platter, and from it, he dispensed advice to the new king for the entirety of his rule, which was long, just, and miserable.

Sankt Lukin is the patron saint of politicians.

# SANKTA MAGDA

There have been many bad years for Ravka, and in one of these bitter years, the crops failed and the cattle died off, leaving the people to starve. As so often happens in these dark times, a woman was accused of being a witch and bringing this desolation upon her village.

Her name was Magda and she had long lived at the edge of town, offering cures and potions of all kinds, delivering babies and feeding them her porridges and tonics when their empty-bellied mothers could give no milk.

She had never taken a husband and had no family to protect her, and her home was on a very nice plot of land much coveted by some of the most powerful leaders of the town. So Magda was not surprised when one of their wives pointed a bony finger at her and accused her of consorting with demons for the sake of making trouble for the good and righteous people of the town.

Magda did not wait to smell the torches being lit. Before the mob could knock down her door, she fled to the woods where she had long gathered herbs and plants to make her cures, and which she knew better than any hunter.

The town leaders congratulated themselves on having rid their village of a witch, and the people rested easier in their beds, sure that their troubles were now over. But rain did not fall in the spring, and frost came early in autumn, and the remaining cattle and sheep had no place to graze, so they sickened and died. Babies—some of whom Magda had delivered—wailed their hunger from their cribs, and mothers smothered their own children to end their suffering.

The town grew restless, the people wild-eyed. As another terrible winter set in, people began to wonder. Perhaps Magda had not been the only witch in their midst. Two sisters were accused of making dark bargains with creatures from the other side—the cold woman who lives at the bottom of the river, the shadow man who is found behind doors.

Lacking the courage to run into the darkness of the woods, the sisters took shelter at home. "Surely our father will protect us," they whispered as they shivered in their narrow beds. "Surely our brothers will."

Instead, their brothers stole their sisters' shoes and their father took away his daughters' coats so they could not run from the house.

The sisters went to their knees and prayed to the Saints for someone to help them, and to their surprise, a vision appeared at their window—it was Magda, though she looked younger than she had when she'd left the town.

"Come," said Magda. "Come with me now and live as free women."

"It is winter," protested the elder sister. "You wish for us to run barefoot in our nightclothes, out into the forest, where we will surely die of the cold? You are a friend to demons, and no holy woman. Go back to the bottom of the river, witch!"

But the younger sister knew that salvation must sometimes come with sacrifice. She recognized Magda as a messenger from the Saints. She begged her older sister to come with her, but when she would not, the younger girl climbed out of the window alone and followed Magda into the night.

The forest floor was damp and hard, and the branches and stones cut into her bare feet. The wind sliced through her nightclothes and she wept for the misery of it.

At last Magda spoke to her. "You weep and your feet bleed. Your skin is blue with cold. Do you wish to turn back?"

The girl shook her head. "I will die in the woods, a free woman in the company of the trees. Better that than the pyre."

As soon as she spoke these words, she felt herself lifted and sped along, her feet no longer touching the forest floor. Before she could blink three times, she was seated inside a hut, beside a fire, wrapped in furs with a pot of soup before her. There were women all around, stoking the coals in the oven, drying herbs, tending to the garden in the light of the moon—a garden that had no business blooming so late in the year.

The girl knew she had come to a place of salvation. She said prayers of thanks and drank her soup.

As for her older sister, the mob came to the house the next morning, and neither her father nor her brothers barred the door. She told them of the witch who had appeared at their window and taken her younger sister away. She pled her purity and righteous soul, but she was still tied to a stake and died upon the flames.

Her father and brothers went into the woods to hunt for Magda and the sister she'd stolen. When night began to fall they smelled baking bread, meat roasting over a fire, figs stewing in wine. They went mad with it, stumbling deeper into the trees, and have never been heard of since. The same fate has befallen many a hunter in those woods.

The village continued to starve no matter how many girls they put to death. But the girls who prayed to Magda would often find themselves swept up and carried into the heart of the forest, and so she is known as the patron saint of abandoned women, as well as bakers.

# SANKT EGMOND

From the time he was a boy, Egmond had a gift for drawing and building. When the church tower in his village began to slump to the side, he found a way to reinforce the foundation beneath it. The next morning, a massive ash tree was found growing beside it, and ever after, Egmond was known to be favored by the Saints—though those who worship Djel like to claim the ash and Egmond as their own.

Egmond could forge metals that never rusted, fashion nails that would never bend, carve stone into fantastical shapes—slender columns that somehow supported mighty beams, spheres of smooth perfection that balanced as if suspended in the air, magical beasts so detailed they seemed about to snarl or take flight. He was called upon by wealthy men and nobles to build their homes, but the results were never what they had commissioned.

Someone would order the construction of a winter palace to be three stories high, at least twelve feet taller than their neighbor's, and with twice as many rooms. Egmond would deliver a house of one hundred rooms, built to look like the thick-tentacled arms of a kraken crushing a ship.

Instead of a silo, he would build a tower of stone branches hung with impossible gems.

Instead of a sensible rectangular schoolhouse, he would build an orb of glass and stone with windows for each student to gaze through that made the surrounding landscape seem alien as a faraway land.

Eventually, one of Egmond's frustrated clients decided he'd had enough. When the grand summer home he'd commissioned turned out to be an orchard of residences built to look like hollowed-out trees—all of them hidden behind an immovable wall of mist—he accused Egmond of fraud. Egmond was thrown into the dungeons of the royal castle, high on the cliffs above Djerholm.

If one had to stay at the castle, the dungeons were actually not a bad place to be. The cells were cold and damp but protected from the wind that blew through the cracks in the walls of the rooms high above.

As the ruthless storms of the Fjerdan coast roared, the princes and princesses, kings and queens huddled by fires they could not keep burning. The storms never paused for breath; they howled and howled, beasts that would never tire. The castle's watchtower toppled. Water poured through the beleaguered roof, pooling in the royal chambers, and the queen woke to see her crown floating down the hall.

The royal family brought engineers and architects to court, but they all had the same thing to say: This place is cursed. Leave the high cliffs and relocate the capital.

The night of Hringkälla, when its rooms should have been full of people drinking and dancing, the castle was nearly empty. All the courtiers who could flee had done so, seeking sanctuary in the town below. All the guests who had been invited had regretfully declined. The wind came wailing off the sea like an infant torn from its mother's breast, and the castle walls swayed to and fro.

"Can no one save us?" cried the king.

"Will no one help us?" wept the queen.

Down in the dungeon, Egmond placed one hand in a puddle of

rainwater and one hand upon the castle wall, where the tiniest tendril of a root had begun to find its way through the gaps in the stone. A great rumbling was heard, and for a moment, it seemed the whole building would fly apart. Then a final thunderous roar echoed through the night, and a massive ash tree shot from the ground up through the very center of the castle.

Silence fell. True silence. The wind had stilled. Rain no longer dripped from the roof. The ash tree's roots had sealed up the floors, crowded through the cracks in the stone, and buttressed the castle walls. Its bark was white and shone like new snow.

A guard had seen what Egmond had done in the dungeons, and he had the prisoner brought before the king and queen.

"Are you the boy who saved our castle?" asked the king.

"Yes," said Egmond. "And if you let me, I will build you a great palace that will stand for all eternity, never to be breached."

"Do this and you will be rewarded," said the king. "Fail us and you will be put to death as a thief and a fraud."

The palace Egmond built was unlike any seen before it. A stone serpent guarded its high towers, its bridge of glass and moat of floating frost, its silver clock tower, and the sacred ash at its heart. Ever since, the Ice Court has stood, its walls unbreached by any army.

Sankt Egmond is the patron saint of architects.

# SANKT ILYA
# IN CHAINS

There was a gifted healer and inventor who lived on the outskirts of a farming village. Ilya was a recluse, happiest to remain in his workshop and keep to himself, but he could be counted on for a tonic or help with a plow when asked. He was only seen in the village when trading his cures or the pelts of animals he had trapped for food. On these rare occasions, he was usually scribbling away frantically in an old leather book.

Once a man asked him, "Ilya, what great wonders are you imagining in those pages?" But Ilya only scowled and continued down the road, eager to return to his experiments. What he hoped to accomplish in his workshop was a mystery, and many suspected that Ilya had long since passed from ambition to madness.

Then, one day, deep in his books and potions, Ilya heard screaming from the fields beyond his home. He followed the terrible sound and found a farmer and his wife wailing over the body of their young son. The child had been nearly cut in half by a plow blade and his blood had soaked into the soil, making a red halo around his body. His eyes were gray and glassy; no breath stirred his chest. No one could recover from such a wound.

But Ilya knelt and, head bent, placed his hands upon what should have been a corpse. To the shock of all who stood watching, the wound seemed to knit together. Moments later the boy's eyes cleared. He blinked. His chest began to rise and fall—in hitches and gasps at first, and then in steady rhythm. The boy sat up and laughed and called to his mother and father to embrace him.

But the child's parents did not go to him. They had seen the extent of his injury. They had seen the life leave his body. Whatever thing smiled and held its arms out to them was not their son.

The villagers who had come running when they heard the mother's cries now stared at this child who should not breathe and the man who had somehow drawn air back into his lungs. It was not natural to make life from death. And they wondered, where had Ilya been when their wives and children and loved ones had suffered? Where was this great healer when Yana's baby was born blue and cold? Or when the firepox had carried off half the village only a few years past? Why had he not appeared when Baba Lera wasted away to nothing, growing weaker with each passing day and praying for death that didn't come until she was little more than a heap of sticks rubbing together her prayer beads?

They seized Ilya and clapped him in heavy chains, a collar for his neck, and fetters for his wrists and ankles. They dragged him to the bridge that overlooked the river, where the water foamed white around the jagged rocks, and they cast Ilya over the side. It is said his corpse emerged on a sandbank many miles south, perfectly preserved and guarded by a white stag, who stood vigil over the body for three full months.

The child Ilya had dragged back from the next world wandered the village, asking for his mother and father, begging for a place to sleep. Every door was closed to him, and so he was left to the woods, where he can still be heard crying.

Sankt Ilya is the patron saint of unlikely cures.

# SANKTA URSULA
# OF THE WAVES

n the northern reaches of Fjerda, a young princess called
Ursula found her way to the worship of the Saints and
prayed each day to them. Those who knelt at the ash altar
of Djel deemed this worship unlawful and demanded she
give up the practice.

She would not. Convinced that her stubborn refusal was
a sure sign she was possessed by some demon, her family
hauled Ursula down to the shore, determined to drive out
the evil spirit that had taken hold of the girl's soul. There,
in the shallows, surrounded by townspeople muttering
prayers to Djel, they held her beneath the water as they beat
the surface of the sea with ash boughs. But as many times as
they dunked her under the waves, and as long as they held
her there, she did not drown or even sputter for breath.

The Fjerdans took this as proof that she had become
host to some unholy power. They claimed she was no longer
a natural girl, but surely half fish, and that she should be cut
open to see if she was truly human.

A knife was brought to shore and given to a priest of
Djel, but before he unsheathed it, he begged Ursula to
renounce her faith and once more honor the Wellspring.
Ursula refused.

Prepared to split her in two and prove she was no longer a human girl but some malevolent scaled thing, the
priest placed the blade of the knife to the hollow of
the princess's throat, when suddenly a cry rang out from

the city's watchtower. The crowd that had gathered on the shore looked far out to sea, and there they saw a wave rushing toward the city, so wide and so high that it blocked the sun. They turned and ran, but there was no escape.

The great wave consumed the city. Just as the priest's blade hand had sought to split Ursula in two, the ocean cut into the shore, sundering it from Fjerda's northern coast and creating the islands known as Kenst Hjerte, the broken heart. Ursula, who had clung resolutely to her faith, survived and lived to an old age in a rock cave on one of the islands, eating nothing but the mussels and oysters she collected from the tide pools, and drinking nothing but salt water.

A chapel was built into the rock on her island, where sailors' wives still come to pray to Ursula, patron saint of those lost at sea. They leave offerings of bread baked into the shape of fish, and wish for their lovers' swift return. When they leave, some find bones or sea pearls in their pockets, though no one is sure if these are ill or good omens.

# SANKT
# MATTHEUS

A beast was terrorizing a town on the edge of the permafrost. Children were snatched right before their mothers' watching eyes, and men were slaughtered in the fields.

Some said the beast was a bear, some a pack of wolves. Others claimed it was a tiger that had escaped a noblewoman's menagerie. The town elders offered a reward and many local hunters went into the woods, but none returned with a pelt to show for their trouble, and many did not return at all.

The townspeople wrote to the king to ask for aid, and he sent the best of his hunters, a giant of a man named Dag Ivar. Ivar and his men arrived in a great procession of coaches, swords, and crossbows. Dressed in heavy coats of wool and velvet and the pelts of beasts they'd slain before, they took up residence in the town's finest home. Ivar and his men swore that they would catch the beast and send its skin back to the king before the winter was out.

But their first venture into the woods was fruitless, as was the second, and the third. The traps they set remained untouched. They followed tracks that seemed to vanish and spent hours walking in circles.

Ivar merely laughed. If the beast wished for a challenge, then a challenge it would have. The hunters dressed as women, since the beast had been known to attack women traveling alone. They tried luring the monster with the still-fresh bodies of its most recent victims. They painted the trees with pig blood.

Days passed and no kill was made. Meanwhile, a young girl went to fetch eggs from the henhouse and was torn apart, pieces of her limbs found in a damp cloud of bloody chicken feathers. Three school-children vanished on their way home—there one moment, then gone, leaving nothing behind but the echoes of their cries.

Soon the townspeople were mocking the great hunter. They stood outside his lodgings, dressed in cheap imitations of his fancy furs and velvet cloak, howling in the early morning hours.

Tired of their abuse, Dag Ivar petitioned the king to return home. These people were heathens and undeserving of the king's attentions; surely the beast that preyed upon them was just punishment for their devilish ways. But the hunter did not receive a letter back. Instead, on the next mail coach, a holy man arrived, a monk known as Mattheus.

"I will go talk to the wolves," he told Dag Ivar, and into the woods he went.

The hunter laughed heartily and promised to bury him with much ceremony—if they could find the remnants of his body. Mattheus had no fear. He knew the Saints went with him.

When the monk had been in the woods less than an hour, he spot-ted a gray shape moving between the trees. The wolf stalked closer, moving in circles, her yellow eyes like sullen moons in the gathering dark. Mattheus did not shy away. He had packed his bag with meat and salt fish, and he offered the wolf food from his own hand.

Now, had he not been so holy, who knows what might have hap-pened. But because he was a good man and beloved by the Saints, the wolf approached and did not simply devour him where he stood. The creature sniffed the meat, cautious lest the food be poisoned, and at last, ate from Mattheus' palm. They sat for awhile, Mattheus feeding the wolf and talking of events from his journey.

After a fair time had passed, he said, "You have eaten many people from the town, and they wish to hunt you to your death."

"They may try," said the wolf.

"I fear the wolfhunter will set fire to the woods to salve his pride."

"What am I to do?" said the wolf. "My children must eat too."

Mattheus had no answer, so he did what he could. Every day, he went into the woods with prayers upon his lips and food in his hands, and every day he sat with the wolf and eventually her pups.

The wolves were well fed and so the killings stopped. The townspeople could till their fields and their children played near the woods without fear.

But the wolfhunter Dag Ivar could not walk down the street without people laughing at him. He ranted and raged, and when he could bear the snickers and jeers no longer, he strode to the center of the town square to denounce Mattheus. He claimed the holy man was in league with the beasts and had drawn them to the village in the first place.

The good people of the village set the hem of the wolfhunter's fine velvet coat alight and chased Dag Ivar down the road and out of town. Mattheus continued to visit with the pups until they were grown wolves themselves. They came when he called, lay at his feet, thumped their tails when he told them stories. Their pups were tame in the very same way, and took to guarding the doorways and hearths of the village their grandmother had once terrorized.

These were the first dogs, and this is why Sankt Mattheus is the patron saint of those who love and care for animals.

# SANKT
# DIMITRI

imitri was the son of a king but wished he had been born otherwise. From his early days, he wanted only to contemplate the works of the Saints and study scripture rather than statecraft.

When the time came for him to assume his responsibilities as a future ruler and to find a bride, he begged his parents' pardon and informed them that he had no intention of marrying or of ever assuming the throne. He would give his life over to piety and prayer.

The king had no other heirs, so he and his wife tried every manner of persuasion—some kind, some cruel—to reach their son. Always, Dimitri met their arguments and attacks with the same calm refusal. He would not take a bride. He would not wear a crown. He would have the life he'd chosen and no other.

At their wits' end, the king and queen ordered their only son locked in a tower, vowing that he would be denied food until he agreed to wed and become the prince he was meant to be. Each day, the queen knocked on the door to the tower, and each day Dimitri told her that he would not come down. She offered him sweets and savories, dishes he'd loved as a child, meats roasted with spices from far-away lands, but Dimitri always replied that he needed no sustenance but faith.

This went on for more than a year. The queen and king were certain the servants were sneaking their son food, so they ordered the door sealed up and guards placed beneath the tower window. No one came or went, and yet still Dimitri refused to emerge.

At last the queen demanded that the tower be opened so that she could see her son. When the guards broke through the door, they found a skeleton sitting at Dimitri's desk. It cheerfully waved to the queen and invited her to pray with him. The queen ran screaming from the tower, and the king and all their servants followed.

Sankt Dimitri, patron saint of scholars, may be praying there still.

# SANKT GERASIM
# THE MISUNDERSTOOD

At a young age, the monk Gerasim took a vow of silence, and he kept to it for over fifty years, never speaking a word. In his seventieth year, he bid his brother monks goodbye and set forth from the monastery where he had lived his entire life. He made a pilgrimage across the True Sea and saw many strange places and extraordinary things.

When he returned, the duke who owned the land where the monastery stood ordered that Gerasim appear before him and tell the court of his journeys and the wonders he had beheld. But Gerasim would not break his vow.

The duke and his wife were not pleased and called for the abbot, who begged Gerasim to speak, telling him that otherwise, the monastery might forfeit the goodwill of their landlord and the monks might lose their home. He promised that the Saints would forgive him for breaking his vow of silence.

But Gerasim had not spoken since he was fifteen. He had been at the monastery many years before the abbot and had long since forgotten the use of his tongue. Still, he did not want his brothers to lose their home. He gestured for paints and brushes to be brought to him, and there, in the grand hall of the duke's home, he painted a mural that stretched from floor to ceiling and wall to wall. It showed the prairies and ports of Novyi Zem, the crowded harbors of Kerch, the mists and stony shores of the Wandering Isle.

It showed creatures of every shape and size, orchards blooming with unfamiliar fruit, men and women in all manner of dress and finery, and in the very last corner, the duke's gracious palace. Gerasim painted himself and the abbot standing before the duke and duchess—both the nobleman and his beautiful wife dressed in gold.

It was said the Saints guided his hand, for no single man could create a work so fine as that. The colors glowed as if lit by sunlight, and the clouds seemed to move across the painted sky.

But in the end the duke and the duchess did not care for the way they had been depicted and ordered Gerasim executed. He died without ever speaking a word, not even to plead for his life.

The monks were commanded to leave their home and the monastery was destroyed, its stones used to build a new wing of the duke's palace. Ten years later, while the duke was hosting a lavish feast, an earthquake struck. Neither the old palace nor the new wing were harmed, not a stone shaken—except for the wall bearing Gerasim's mural. It collapsed, killing the duke and the duchess and all their guests, burying them beneath the old monk's wonders.

Gerasim is known as the patron saint of artists.

# SANKTA ALINA
# OF THE FOLD

A countess lost her husband in one of Ravka's many wars. He'd been a high-ranking officer and should have remained far from the fighting, but emboldened by drink, he'd ridden his great white stallion along the front, taunting the enemy, looking for a fight. He'd gotten a bullet to the head instead. His horse had been found many miles from the battlefield, grazing beside a gentle stream. The nobleman was found there too, long since dead, his body hanging from the saddle, one foot still caught in a stirrup.

The countess buried her husband, and as was fashionable in some circles, she decided to convert her summer home into an orphanage for the many children left parentless in times of war. The house was painted palest apricot, its roofline and windows edged in gold leaf. From its rose gardens, you could see the wide stretch of a lake and the other elegant homes dotting its shores and, in the distance, the thick forests of the lower Petrazoi.

The orphans came to this magical place covered in dirt and lice, and those from the border towns arrived with ghosts in tow—memories of raids in the night, homes set to the torch, mothers and fathers gone suddenly silent and cold. The pretty house on the lake seemed an impossible haven full of good food and watched over by a beautiful new mother who wiped their faces clean and dressed them in new clothes.

It was true that they were made to work for their keep, but that was to be expected. The countess had no servants, and so it was left to the children to scrub the floors, stoke the fires, tend the garden, mend the clothes, prepare and serve the meals. The children were to tell no one of the work they did.

Once a week, the countess would dress her favorite orphans in matching apricot velvet and they would pile into the elegant boat she kept moored at her private dock. They would row out to the center of the lake, where all the residents of the elegant summer homes would gather to drink champagne and gossip. The children would sing when commanded to and tell of their wonderful, pampered lives when asked. "How lucky you are!" the noblewoman's friends would say, and the children, desperate to please their new mother, would agree.

But at night, huddled in their beds in the dormitory, they would whisper to each other, *Be careful. Be careful. Or Mother will take you to the garden.* Because when a child displeased her or sang off-key or complained that he was hungry, sometimes that child would vanish in the middle of the night.

"Loving parents came to claim little Anya!" the countess said one day when Anya was gone from her bed. "Now do not make me wait for my bathwater."

Klava did not believe a word of it. In the night she'd woken, roused by some sound, and gone to the window. Amid the roses, she'd seen the countess with a lantern in hand, leading Anya down past the hedge maze to a door in the garden wall. This was the way with all the orphans who disappeared.

The truth was that the countess had no money. She hadn't the means to pay servants or keep up the house. She certainly didn't have the money to feed a dozen orphans. And so, occasionally, she would sell one off to a wool merchant who traded frequently with Ketterdam in both legal and illegal goods. She didn't know where the children went and she didn't worry too much over it. The wool merchant seemed a kindly sort, and he paid well.

Little Klava knew none of this. But she knew that loving parents did not skulk about like thieves to fetch their children under cover of darkness. And no one was ever permitted at the apricot house, so how would anybody have seen Anya or the other children and decided to claim them? She felt certain that whatever happened beyond the garden wall was not good.

Summer dragged on and the sun beat down on the grounds of the apricot house, turning the roses brown. The noblewoman's mood grew more prickly as she sweated through her gowns. She took the orphans out to the lake less and less. "You're boring," she told them. "Why would my friends want to see you again?"

One morning, three new children arrived at the orphanage—two brothers and a sister, all with silvery blond hair and leaf green eyes. "How alike you are!" the countess exclaimed, happy for the first time in weeks. "Like little dolls. We must have you fitted for new clothes and take you out on the lake."

Klava watched as the countess turned her cold gaze on the other orphans, the boring, tiresome orphans who did nothing but eat her food and disappoint her. Klava knew it was time to run.

That night, when the house was dark and quiet, Klava told the other orphans she intended to escape the noblewoman's house.

"Where will you go?" they asked. "What will you do?"

"I'll find work," Klava replied. "I'll live in the woods and eat berries, but I won't wait for her to make me vanish. I only need to reach the other side of the forest. There's an old farmhouse there and a widow who knew my parents. She will help me."

Klava urged them to come with her. She warned the pretty new children that the noblewoman would one day tire of them too. In the end, they decided they would all make their escape.

Out the window the orphans went, one by one, dressed in their apricot velvet, bundled in the blankets from their beds. They went out to the lake and piled into the boat, and they rowed it across the water to the woods. But just as they were entering the trees, they heard shouts of alarm, the barking of dogs. The countess had discovered they were missing.

The children ran, deeper and deeper into the woods, the night crowding in around them as branches snagged their clothing and thorns stung their skin. Klava pushed on, her heart pounding and tears in her eyes, sure there would be no mercy if they were caught, terrified that she had led her friends to their doom—for the darkness was impenetrable now and she knew she had lost her way. They would never reach the other side of the forest. They would never find the farmhouse and salvation.

Through her panting breaths, she prayed to Sankta Alina, a defiant girl, an orphan herself, who had driven back the darkness of the Fold and united Ravka. "Alina the Bright," she whispered, "daughter of Keramzin, slayer of monsters, save us."

No sound came, no gentle words of guidance, no chorus of trumpets to lead them on, but through the trees, the orphans saw a gleam of light—violet and blue, red, green, and gold: a rainbow in the night.

Klava followed the arc of the rainbow through the darkness and on to the farmhouse, where the orphans pounded on the door and woke the old widow who lived there. She was startled but happy to see Klava, and she welcomed them all inside. She hid the orphans in the root cellar, and when the countess arrived with her dogs, the widow said she had seen no one the whole night and had been sleeping soundly. The countess was, of course, free to search the property.

The hounds whined and the noblewoman ranted, but the orphans were nowhere to be found. The countess was forced to return to her empty summer home, and without free labor to maintain it, the place soon fell into disrepair, the rosebushes inching closer and closer until they had consumed the house entirely. It's said the countess was trapped inside and became more thorns than woman.

Some of the orphans journeyed from the farmhouse to seek their fortunes elsewhere, but Klava stayed to help the widow work her fields, and each night she said prayers of thanks to Sankta Alina, patron saint of orphans and those with undiscovered gifts.

# THE STARLESS SAINT

A young man lived in Novokribirsk, on the very border of the Shadow Fold. His name was Yuri, and his parents had sent him to live with his uncle, where he could work on the dry docks and make some kind of living. Truth be told, they were delighted their peculiar son had found employment. Yuri had taught himself to read and seemed happiest in communion with the texts he borrowed from anyone willing to lend him a book. While his parents thought it was all well and good to talk of myths and fables and tales from the past, none of that would pay the rent, and they feared Yuri would talk his way into a monastery, leaving his parents to the mercy of time and age.

The work in Novokribirsk did not suit Yuri. He was tall enough, but narrow as a willow switch. His eyesight was poor and he had always been clumsy. The strong men who worked the dry docks—building and repairing sandskiffs, loading and unloading cargo—mocked Yuri's fumbling ways, the wheezing of his narrow chest, the fogged lenses of his glasses.

It might not have been so bad if Yuri's uncle had some patience or kindness in him, but he was the worst of them. When Yuri dropped a box or lagged behind the other workers, his uncle would smack him hard across the back of his head. When Yuri's mumbled prayers disturbed him, he'd stick out a foot and Yuri would go tumbling. At home, his uncle's hands often became closed fists. He laughed when

Yuri walked to church on Sundays and said the Saints had no interest in a man who could not work for a living.

But Yuri knew the Saints were watching. Each morning and each night, he prayed to them and vowed to give his life over to their worship if they would only free him from his uncle's cruelty and let him devote his life to study. During the long days working the docks, he whispered psalms and prayers to himself, and in Novokribirsk's grand chapel, he endeavored to teach himself liturgical Ravkan. In the quiet of the church's little library, he would lose himself in the old stories of the Saints, his fingers turning the pages in a kind of meditation, the shadows creeping over his shoulders.

One evening, Yuri had drifted so deeply into the comfort of words, he didn't realize that night had fallen and the shadows had pooled around his feet. He ran home but was late getting supper on the table, and Yuri's uncle beat his nephew until his fists were tired.

In the morning, Yuri could not rise from his bed. His eyes were nearly swollen shut and his aching body felt as if it had been sewn together by a careless hand, the stitches pulling at every joint. His uncle left for work on the dry docks and vowed that if Yuri did not meet him there, another beating would be waiting that night. Yuri knew he would not survive it.

He dragged himself across the floor. He forced himself to dress and eat a bit of porridge. He limped down the street to the town square. Yuri knew he had to keep moving, but as he leaned against the fountain at the town's center, trying to summon his strength, he heard a voice whisper to him, *Do not go.*

Yuri didn't know if the voice was real, only that he couldn't move his feet another step.

*My uncle will find me here*, he thought, *and this is where I will die. For* he knew that no one would intervene. They never had before. In the long months Yuri had been in Novokribirsk, they had always turned away, pretending not to see his bruises or hear his cries. *The old man is harmless*, they said. *Some boys need more discipline than others.*

Yuri looked down the street to where the dry docks stood, the Fold a high wall of seething shadow beyond it. He had to move, but again he heard the voice telling him, *Do not go.*

That was when the shadows seemed to move. The Fold shifted and swelled as if it were gathering breath, and then it was rushing toward him, a wall of darkness. It swallowed the dry docks, the buildings beyond. It flooded over the houses of Novokribirsk. Yuri heard screaming all around him, but he was unafraid.

The shadow tide rushed all the way up to the toes of Yuri's boots, and there it stopped. He could hear the weeping of people trapped inside the Fold, their sudden agony as they were torn apart by volcra. He wondered briefly if he could hear his uncle. Then he fell upon his knees and gave thanks to the darkness.

That day, half of Novokribirsk was lost when the Darkling expanded the Fold. Many cursed the man responsible for this cruelty and celebrated his death when it finally came. But there are others who worship him still, the Starless One, patron saint of those who seek salvation in the dark.

# SAINT OF THE BOOK

I don't remember my own story.

I may have slept in a hayloft or on a featherbed.

I may have eaten from silver dishes or stolen scraps from the kitchen.

I may have worn summer silks and jewels in my hair.

Or maybe I went barefoot and clawed in the dirt, searching for roots, for gold, for shelter. I can't recall. There have been too many stories in between, miracles and martyrdoms, too much blood spilled, too much ink. There was a war. There were a thousand wars. I knew a killer. I knew a hero. They might have been the same man. I remember only how I fell into books, never to rise from their pages, how I was never truly awake until I began to dream of other worlds.

I wander now, lost among the shelves. My hand cramps around the pen. I gather dust. But someone has to set down the words, put them in the proper order. I am the library and the librarian, hoarding lives, a catalog for the faithful.

Erase my name. *Indelible* is a word for stories.

# ENTER THE GRISHAVERSE

## The Shadow and Bone Trilogy

## The Six of Crows Duology